Written by: Norah Cave
Illustrated by: Brit Cave
Book Design by: Brandon Cave

Adventures of Link:
Helper Hero

Copyright ©2022 Healey Creative, LLC
All rights reserved. Published by Healey Creative. Associated logos and designs are copyright of Healey Creative.

The publisher does not have any control over or assume any responsibility for third party websites and their content.

No part of this publication may be reproduced, stored in a retrieval system, or transmitted in any form or by any means, electronic, mechanical, photocopying, recording, or otherwise, without written permission of the publisher.

This book is a work of fiction. Names, characters, places, and incidents are either the product of the author's imagination or are used fictitiously, and any resemblance to actual persons, living or dead, business establishments, events, or locales is entirely coincidental.

First printed in 2022.

Dedicated to my family.
- Norah

Hi! My name is Link!

I love playing superheroes!

I want to be a superhero some day!

I like to play superheroes when I help my dog get her toy from under the couch.

I pretend I am saving Mr. Cluckles from the dark cave of my enemy!

I like to play superheroes when I help Grandma bake cookies.

I pick out the egg shells to save us from crunchy cookies, like a hero protects their friends!

I am friendly in my neighborhood to all the kids.

I like to play and share with kindness just like my heroes do!

I like to play superheros
all the time.

Maybe helping my friends and
family is my superpower!
It could be yours too!

I think there is a superhero
in all of us!

What's your superhero name?

_____

How can you be a superhero today?

_____

_____

_____

Tape a picture of your superhero on this page!

Copyright ©2022 Healey Creative, LLC
All rights reserved. Published by Healey Creative. Associated logos and designs are copyright of Healey Creative.

The publisher does not have any control over or assume any responsibility for third party websites and their content.

No part of this publication may be reproduced, stored in a retrieval system, or transmitted in any form or by any means, electronic, mechanical, photocopying, recording, or otherwise, without written permission of the publisher.

This book is a work of fiction. Names, characters, places, and incidents are either the product of the author's imagination or are used fictitiously, and any resemblance to actual persons, living or dead, business establishments, events, or locales is entirely coincidental.

First printed in 2022.

Made in United States
Orlando, FL
04 March 2024

44409114R00015